Tales From a Magical Forest

Written by Justin Frank Trzaskos

Illustrated by Irina Zatica Trzaskos

Tales From a Magical Forest

FIRST EDITION

ISBN-9781794553002

This book belongs to:

By order of Queen Grace and King Noble, the owner of this book may enter the Magical Forest at any time.

Enjoy the adventure!

Tales From a Magical Forest

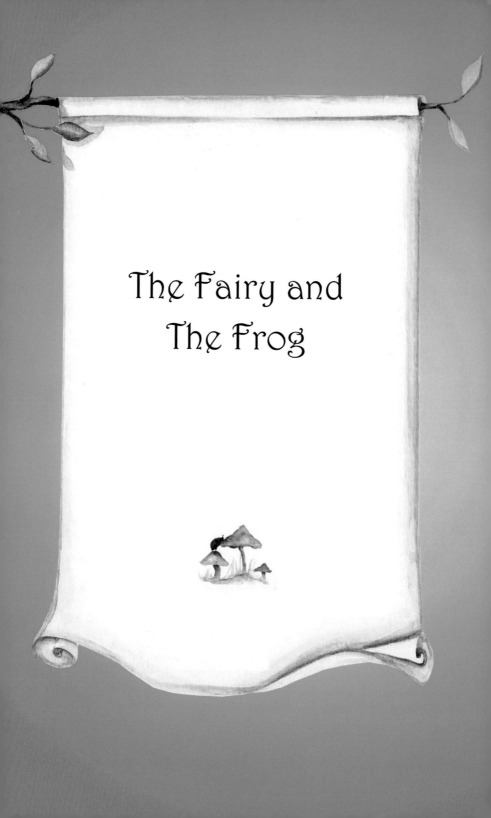

The Fairy and The Frog

Once upon a time, deep in the woods, there was a pond.

The pond was home to plants, fish, dragonflies and frogs.

Each spring, the frogs would lay their eggs and tadpoles would hatch.

One day, a very special tadpole was born, but he did not think he was special.

When the tadpole grew arms and legs, he was not happy either.

His brothers and sisters were all very happy to live in the pond, deep in the forest. But he wasn't.

The frog decided to hop away and find a new home.

He leaped out of the pond, plopped into the stream nearby and began to float away.

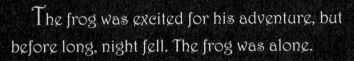

The frog was excited for his adventure, but before long, night fell. The frog was alone.

The sounds of the forest made him scared. The frog decided to hide in a hole for the night.

In the morning, he was ready to continue his adventure.

He floated down the stream, enjoying the sun and the breeze.

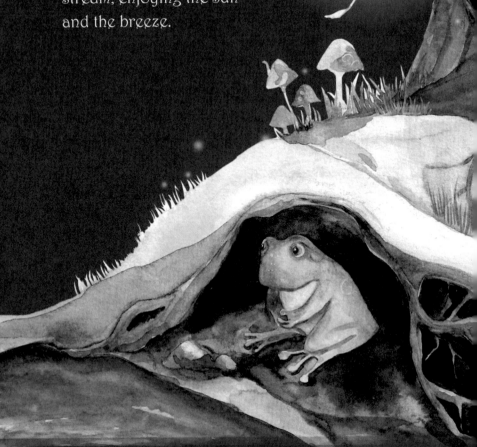

In the afternoon, the frog saw a small boy crying by the side of the stream. The boy had wings.

Drying his eyes, the boy asked the frog, "Will you help me?"

"I can try," said the frog, "but I am just an ordinary frog. What can I do?"

"I am just an ordinary fairy," said the boy. "My wing is hurt, and I could really use a ride down the stream. Will you help me?"

The small fairy looked very upset.

"I dropped my bag then hit a tree. I've lost my things," he said.

"Climb on my back," said the frog. "I will give you a ride."

"Thank you, thank you," said the fairy.

The two began to travel down the stream.

As they floated along, the fairy asked, "Where are you going?"

"I'm moving away from home because I do not like being a frog," said the frog, softly.

"Everyone has something special to offer. You just don't know what it is yet. I think that being a frog would be great," said the fairy.

The frog let out a loud **CROAK** to laugh at the fairy.

After floating a bit, the fairy asked to stop.

"This is where I dropped my things."

The fairy looked around and could see his bag at the bottom of the stream.

"Oh no!"

"What's wrong? You have found your bag," said the frog.

"It's at the bottom of the stream, and I can't swim well. I usually fly," replied the fairy.

"Don't worry, I'll be right back."

Then the frog was gone with a splash and dove under the water. A moment later, he came back with the bag in his mouth.

"Here you go," said the frog.

"Thank you, thank you. You are an exceptional frog!"

"It's nothing," said the frog "It's easy for me."

"I suppose I will continue down the stream," said the frog. "Goodbye!"

"Wait, wait," yelled the fairy. "Wait for me! I need your help! My home is down the stream, too. If you take me there, you can have some food and rest for the night."

The fairy said, "You can meet my friends and family. They would love to meet a frog like you."

"Did you say a frog like me? What is so special about me?" The frog frowned.

The fairy laid a hand on the frog's shoulder. "Of course you are special! If you do not believe me, you should come with me. I will show you a magical pond where you can see a reflection of your true self—who you are meant to be."

"I *am* hungry," groaned the frog, licking his lips. "And I am curious, too. Hop on my back."

The two companions began to travel again down the stream, enjoying the sunny day.

After a while, they came to a pile of stones blocking the way. "We're stuck," said the fairy.

"Just jump," said the frog.

"I can't jump that high! I usually fly," said the fairy.

"No problem," said the frog. "Hold on tight!" He leaped over the rocks and landed on the other side.

"You're the best," said the fairy, to the frog.

Just around twilight, the two heard the distant twinkling of bells.

"We're almost home," yelled the fairy.

As they turned a corner in the stream, they could see a beautiful tree filled with lights and little fairy homes. The lights and the colors were all reflected in the magical pond that surrounded the marvelous tree.

"We made it," shouted the two friends.

"Thank you, my friend," said the boy. "I will tell the Queen Fairy how you helped me. She will take you to the magical pond to see your reflection."

The frog let out a loud croak of joy.

Later that evening, after a delicious dinner, the boy brought the frog to the Queen Fairy.

"Thank you, kind frog, for saving my little friend. He has told me of your great bravery and abilities," said the Queen Fairy.

"You may now look into the magical pond and see your true reflection."

The frog hopped to the edge of the pond and gazed into the still waters. He stared and he stared, but all he saw was his own reflection. He appeared no different than he was.

"I don't understand," said the frog, sadly. "I am looking at myself."

"Yes. It *is* you. The reflection I see is of a brave frog who helped my hurt fairy float down the stream, dove underwater and jumped over large rocks. These are very impressive skills. You are exactly who you should be," said the Queen Fairy.

The frog did not realize that helping the boy meant so much.

"Tonight we will celebrate in your honor because you are a hero to our village. You may stay here as long as you wish. You are now an honorary fairy," the boy told the frog when he came back from the pond.

The fairies danced and sang to celebrate the frog who saved their brother.

"Thanks again for saving me," said the boy quietly to the frog. "I guess you were supposed to be a frog, after all. If you need a break from the pond, you will always be an honorary fairy. You can visit our village any time that you wish."

"Thank you, my friend," said the frog, "but I think I will return to my pond to see my family tomorrow."

"Ok, Ok," laughed the fairy. "Do you want some company? I could use some adventure while my wing finishes healing."

The frog let out another huge **CROAK** of laughter. "Yes, of course, a frog needs a friend to make the adventure more exciting. Let's go! "

The two friends jumped back into the
stream. They swam and splashed together,
and when the fairy was tired, he rode on the
frog's back. Throughout the journey to the
frog's pond, they talked and laughed. The
two were friends from then on.

Even now, years later, the story is still
told at both the fairy village and the big pond
about how a fairy and a frog became best
friends.

The Fairy and
The Bird

Once upon a time, deep in a magical forest, there lived a bird.

The bird loved to fly through the air on sunny days.

She also loved to sing beautiful songs that filled the forest with music.

The bird had colorful feathers and was well known to the forest creatures for her singing.

She would sit on a branch and perform songs for her animal friends.

One day as the bird was flying, she heard someone singing.

She realized the song was coming from high in the sky.

She searched and searched but could not find who the singer was.

"There are not many musicians in the forest," thought the bird. "I hope to find who it is."

A few days later as the bird was singing for the rabbit and turtle, they heard the sound. It seemed to be getting closer.

The animals looked up as the sound got louder.

All of a sudden, a fairy swooped in and landed on the branch.

She threw her hands in the air and let out a long musical note in a grand fashion.

"Do, re, me, fa, so, la-la-la, ti, do," sang the fairy.

The rabbit and turtle applauded. The rabbit clapped very fast, and the turtle clapped very slowly.

The bird was too shocked to clap at all. She thought fairies were only imaginary.

"That was beautiful," said the bird. "I've never met any fairy before, much less a singing one. It was you that I heard."

"I've been looking for you, too," said the fairy "I wanted a friend to sing with. Let's' sing together!"

"Really?" That would be great," chirped the bird.

All afternoon, the two singers performed for the turtle and the rabbit. Other forest animals came to listen, too.

The fairy and the bird became good friends and became very popular for their concerts.

Everyone loved them - except for one mysterious animal that lived in the darkest part of the woods.

As the bird and fairy were singing one day, they heard horrible noises coming from the dark part of the forest.

The rabbit scurried away, and the turtle hid in his shell.

The fairy and the bird flew away and burrowed into the bird's nest.

Every time the two would sing, the terrible noise would start and everyone would leave.

The noise was becoming a problem because the bird and the fairy couldn't finish a single concert.

They decided that the next time they sang, they would stay on the branch — even if the noise started. They would wait bravely and watch for whatever was coming from the dark part of the forest.

Sure enough, the next time they sang, the noise started again. Even though they were frightened, they kept singing as the noise got closer and closer.

Eventually, they could see the reflection of two yellow eyes in the darkness of the forest. The fairy and the bird held each other in fright.

Out hobbled an old crow squawking to the music.

She croaked, "Did I miss the show again?"

"Kaw, kaw, kaw" said the old crow "I want to sing, too!"

The fairy and the bird realized the horrible noise was just an old crow who wanted to sing along.

"I love to sing," shrieked the old crow "Kaw, kaw, what's our next song?"

The bird and the fairy did not want to tell the crow she was not a good singer.

So the crow joined into the beautiful song with a loud "Kawwwww!"

It sounded awful but the fairy and the bird were too polite to say a word.

When they were done singing, the crow said, "Thank you, I have not had any friends in years and have been alone in the dark part of the forest. You have truly made this old crow very happy."

The fairy and the bird invited the crow to join them anytime. The other animals joined in the singing, too.

The rabbit sang and pounded his feet quickly, while the turtle sang and drummed slowly on a stump.

The old crow added in with her loud "Kawwww" whenever she wanted.

The fairy, bird, turtle, rabbit and crow
had a great time singing and laughing.
They did not care that the crow could
not sing or that the rabbit drummed
faster than the turtle. All that mattered
was that they were all having fun.

The entire forest was filled with music. Some of the notes were beautiful, and some were not.

But the joy that the music brought to the group of friends was the most beautiful song of all.

Welcome

to

Camp Summerberry

The first day of summer camp had finally arrived. The animals were excited for their first year at Camp Summerberry.

Mr. Sterling, a grey-haired beaver was the group's leader. Ryker, the fox; Flynn, the cardinal; Abner, the raccoon; and Musky, the skunk, eagerly reported for orientation.

"Listen well, campers," announced Mr. Sterling. "I'm going to teach you everything you need to know about camping. I'm an experienced professional." Mr. Sterling puffed out his chest and proudly proclaimed that he knew every rock, tree and trail of Camp Summerberry. He had camped there since he was young.

"Grab your gear, and let's set up camp. There's much to learn," declared Mr. Sterling. The animals followed their leader to a campsite near the top of a big hill. Ryker and Flynn set up a tent, while Musky and Abner arranged the cooking supplies. Once their things were organized, they regrouped with Mr. Sterling.

"Gather 'round, young ones," said Mr. Sterling, as he reached for a piece of rope to demonstrate how to tie a knot.

"It's time to teach you how to tie a beaver-line knot. See here, the rabbit climbs out of his hole, runs around the tree, past the briar patch and hops over the stump." The young animals followed along, mimicking Mr. Sterling.

"Very good, practice that," yawned Mr. Sterling, as he leaned back against a maple tree. "Past the briar patch, over the stump," he said slowly as he fell asleep. The animals looked at each other and chuckled as Mr. Sterling began to snore.

"Let's go for a hike," said Ryker. "I'm ready for some exploring."

"Ask Mr. Sterling," said Musky.

Flynn flew over to Mr. Sterling and landed on his shoulder. "May we go exploring in the woods?" he asked.

"Huh? Yes, yes, stay together, and remember your training," muttered Mr. Sterling as he opened one eye, still half asleep.

"Let's go," said Abner.

The four young animals walked into the woods. They were enjoying the sights and sounds of nature.

"I know a thing or two about camping," said Ryker. "I can help you learn." Flynn, Abner and Musky listened to Ryker as they walked. He taught them about trees and stars. Also, he said that finding clean water was very important.

"I still have a lot to learn," admitted Ryker. "But we can all learn together!"

The group found a small stream and decided to follow it. It was fun to jump across to the other side and to watch the stream as the water flowed around the mossy rocks. Before long, they became hungry. They wished they had brought a snack.

"Leave it to me," exclaimed Abner. "I'm an excellent cook. Will you help me find a few ingredients? Abner led the group, collecting food from the ground, trees and even the water. The animals sat and looked on while the clever raccoon prepared a meal.

"Today we will be enjoying a cattail, crabapple and Queen Anne's lace soup, followed by a light dandelion and clover salad," said Abner.

"Please also enjoy a refreshing glass of white pine, birch bark and blackberry tea."

"Any skunk cabbage?" Musky looked hopeful.

"Sorry, Musky, skunk cabbage is out of season. We can have some in the spring," replied Abner.

The four animals lost track of time while enjoying their meal. They did not notice a dark storm cloud that quickly approached.

"Uh oh," said Musky, nervously. "Looks like a storm. I can help make a shelter."

Skunks are very good at finding shelter, and it wasn't long before Musky found the perfect den so the friends could stay protected from the rain.

"Thank you, Musky," said Flynn. "It's a lovely den."

Musky's den did have a distinct scent. The group did not complain as each animal was happy to stay dry. Before long, the rain clouds passed, and the group continued on.

"We should go back soon," said Abner. "Mr. Sterling will be worried about us."

"I seem to have lost my direction," said Ryker.

"Leave it to me," proclaimed Flynn. "I can find the way home."

Flynn flew up, above the trees and found the campsite. The group traveled along the stream, retracing the way they came. On the walk, the animals talked about how much they did. They were excited about their shelter, the delicious meal they ate and finding their way home. The friends agreed that they made a great team and that, together, they could do much more.

The hike seemed like it took all day
and the group was ready to rest.
They dragged themselves back into
the campsite and sat down. Mr.
Sterling started to grunt and groan as
he woke from his nap.

"Where were we? Ah yes, the
beaver-line knot. The rabbit comes

out of his hole, around the tree." It was clear that Mr. Sterling did not remember Flynn asking for permission to go exploring.

As the wise beaver continued his lecture, the young animals' eyes started to close. They were exhausted from the adventure and were falling asleep. Musky dozed off first, followed by Abner, then Flynn. Just as Ryker's eyes shut, a loud noise startled them all awake.

"Wake up, sleepy heads, enough class time for you," proclaimed Mr. Sterling. "You can't learn everything about camping from just listening to me! I already have all the answers. You have to learn something for yourselves. Get up and get out there. There is an entire forest to explore! Be back by dinner."

The fox, raccoon, cardinal and skunk spent the rest of the day exploring the camp. They swam in the lake and ran in the field. When they were tired, they practiced the beaver-line knot.

Soon the sun was starting to sink behind the tall treetops, and the friends could hear the other campers gathering for dinner. They enjoyed a great meal cooked by Mr. Sterling. In the evening, the young animals sat by a campfire and talked about all the fun they had.

When it was bedtime, the four friends stumbled into their tents and nestled in their sleeping bags. In the quiet dark, Musky whispered, "Today was a great day, wasn't it?"

Ryker answered, "It was. I wonder what we'll do tomorrow."

"We're going to be experts at camping, just like Mr. Sterling," Said Flynn.

"Musky, can you show me how to find a den," asked Abner.

"Sure, if you can teach me how to cook," answered Musky. "Today was the best day ever."

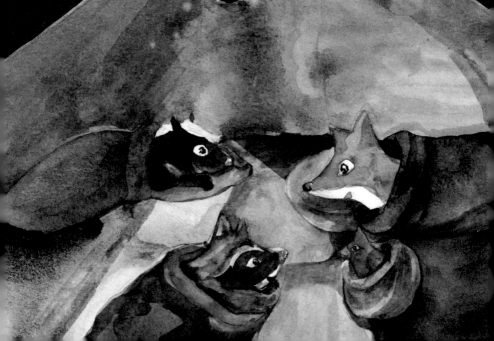

The Fairy and
The Mouse

Once upon a time, in a
magical forest, there lived a
mouse.

The mouse's home was beneath
an old oak tree just a short
distance from a fairy village.
Inside the house, the mouse lived
quite comfortably. The home was
decorated with things found in
the forest.

A storage area held a food supply of acorns for the winter. The mouse's oven was made from small stones, his chairs from carved pinecones and his table from branches. His pictures were painted on white birch bark and framed with twigs. The mouse was quite clever.

Each day, the mouse would scurry about, collecting acorns and building materials. The mouse was an expert in this field and very proud of his home. The mouse hoped, some day, to have a visitor.

One afternoon, just after he returned from the forest, he heard a loud yell of excitement. The mouse could hear the sound getting closer.

With a flash, something fell through the tree and landed with a thump. Oak leaves fluttered from the tree to the ground.

The mouse ran in through his doorway, frightened. As he peered back outside, a dazed fairy climbed from a pile of leaves. "That was great," said the fairy. "But where am I?" The fairy glanced up and saw the mouse hiding by the door. The fairy was very happy to see the mouse and marched right over to the front door.

"Hello, how are you? Do you live here? Where am I?" The mouse's eyes grew large. He had hoped for a visitor but did not expect that visitor to be a fairy who fell from the sky and spouted questions at him. Even so, the mouse was glad to have a guest and asked the fairy please to come inside. The mouse and the fairy went into the kitchen for a cup of tea.

"Please sit and rest," said the mouse. "You certainly made an entrance."

"I'm Dizzy," said the fairy.

"I'm sure you are," replied the mouse. "That was quite a landing."

"No, no, my name is Dizzy, pleased to meet you. I'm an aerial acrobat," said the fairy. "I can fly farther than a bee and faster than a bat. I was experimenting with a new trick and must have made an error in my calculations."

"My word," said the mouse.
"That's quite exciting. I spend most
of my days collecting and
decorating. My name is Fuzzy."

"It's a lovely home, I love it here,"
said the fairy. "The open air is my
home," said the fairy with a heroic
look on his face.

The fairy and the mouse spent the evening talking. The mouse talked about the treasures he finds in the forest and how he uses them. The topic of sticks versus twigs took an hour alone. The fairy shared stories of his flying adventures. He told of the view from the air and the feeling of soaring like a bird. Dizzy and Fuzzy were both very interested in the other's life. It was clear that the two had much to learn from one another.

In the morning, the mouse woke up to find the fairy was gone. He was upset that his new friend had left. He went outside to begin his day of collecting acorns. Much to his surprise, the fairy was outside gathering acorns, seeds and twigs.

"How's this?"

"Incredible," replied the mouse. "You have finished my work for today!"

"I have an idea of how to spend the time," said the fairy. "I woke up early and built something, we're going flying!"

The fairy had made a flying machine from leaves, acorns and twigs, using the building material suggestions the mouse made the night before. The flying machine had a basket, made of twigs and straw. The basket attached to wings, made from bird feathers and leaves.

The aircraft had a handle at the top,
which the fairy held to carry the machine.
The fairy explained that his aircraft
design was quite complicated and would
surely glide in the air.

"You better wear this anyway," said the fairy, handing the mouse a small helmet, made from an acorn top.

"Hop in," shouted the fairy. "Let's take a ride."

The mouse climbed aboard and the fairy lifted the machine into the air. The leaves helped the fairy lift the mouse and glide with the wind. Handmade rope was attached to acorns. The wind spun feathers that attached to the acorns and moved a rope in circles.

The moving rope made the leaves and feathers move up and down. With the fairy's design and a touch of magic, the machine worked! The fairy grabbed the handle and lifted the machine into the air. The wind spun the feathers in circles and the wings began to flap up and down. The mouse wasn't quite sure if the machine was really working or it was just the fairy's magic and pulling, that was lifting him into the air.

For the first time, the mouse saw the whole forest. From the air, they could see the fairy village, the big pond, the stream and waterfalls.

"What a beautiful forest!" said the mouse. "Let's fly over that hill!"

"Hang on!" screamed the fairy, over the noise of the wind.

The fairy pulled the flying machine higher and higher. The mouse held on to the basket with all of his might. The mouse was not used to flying with an aerial acrobat, but he was enjoying every minute. The fairy and the mouse spent the afternoon zipping through the forest. They flew under branches, between trees and over hills. They saw butterflies and birds, gliding in the air, who all looked quite puzzled to see a flying mouse.

"This is wonderful," said the mouse. "I never imagined that I would fly. Thank you!"

At one point, the mouse turned his head and saw Dizzy flying along next to him. He was zipping along in circles, flying up and down and upside down. The mouse looked out of the basket and saw the wings moving and feathers spinning. The machine was working on its own.

"Don't worry," said Dizzy. "I added a little extra magic before I let go. I promise a gentle landing."

After Fuzzy's solo flight, Dizzy grabbed the handle and guided the craft back to the old oak tree. He slowly lowered the basket to the ground, and it landed softly on the moss.

"Touchdown," shouted Dizzy.

After the flight, the two friends returned to the mouse's home. They sat once again and drank tea in the kitchen. But this night, the fairy explained the best materials in the forest for building while the mouse told of his adventures flying.

A Fairy

Christmas Eve

The Christmas Eve,

that I remember best,

was when I stumbled down a hill,

into a fairy winter-fest.

'Twas last Christmas Eve,

as snow softly fell.

I got lost in the woods,

now there's a story to tell.

Just past the nearby town,

down a quiet little street,

up a mountain and back down,

lay something rather neat.

I did not trust my sight

as the forest gleamed with light,

a fairy village filled with life that

brightened up the night.

I could not believe my eyes.

I surely needed rest,

as fairies flew to welcome me

and join them as their guest.

The smell of apples baking

floated in the air.

The sounds of fairy music

echoed everywhere.

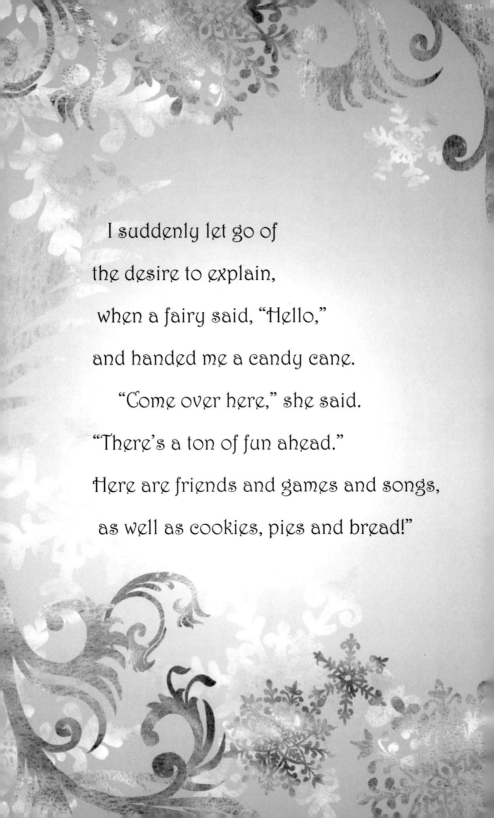

I suddenly let go of

the desire to explain,

 when a fairy said, "Hello,"

and handed me a candy cane.

 "Come over here," she said.

"There's a ton of fun ahead."

Here are friends and games and songs,

 as well as cookies, pies and bread!"

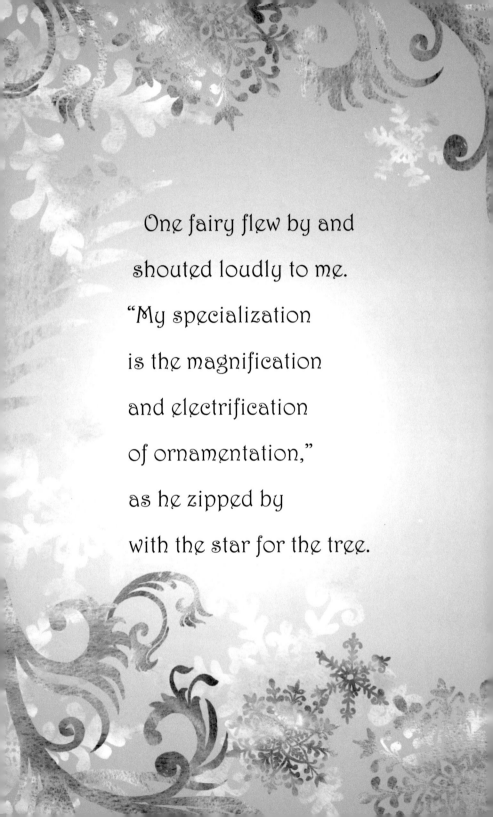

One fairy flew by and

shouted loudly to me.

"My specialization

is the magnification

and electrification

of ornamentation,"

as he zipped by

with the star for the tree.

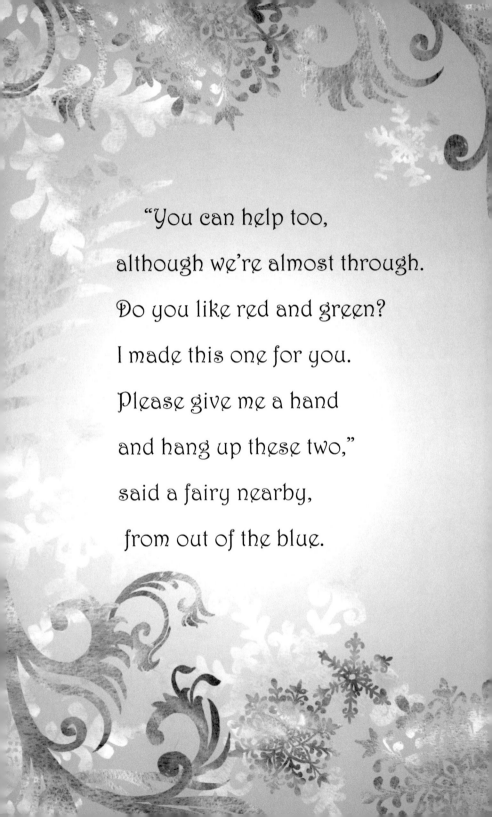

"You can help too,

although we're almost through.

Do you like red and green?

I made this one for you.

Please give me a hand

and hang up these two,"

said a fairy nearby,

from out of the blue.

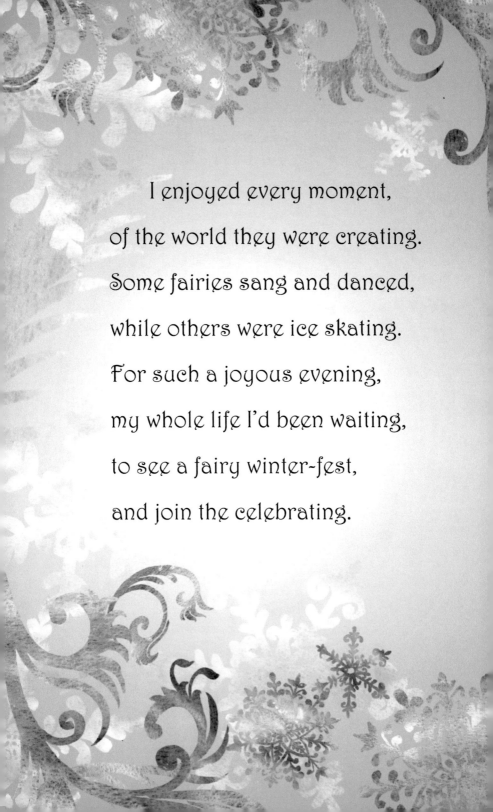

I enjoyed every moment,

of the world they were creating.

Some fairies sang and danced,

while others were ice skating.

For such a joyous evening,

my whole life I'd been waiting,

to see a fairy winter-fest,

and join the celebrating.

I heard "Follow me,

dear sir, if you please.

It's time for our feast filled

with tea, cake and cheese."

The fairy slid by and

I felt a breeze as

she raced down the hill,

on her candy cane skis.

The gathering was splendid,

as I enjoyed the feast.

Nothing short of fascinating

and that's to say the least.

The ending of the evening,

inspired me the most

as the Fairy King and Queen

led the celebration toast.

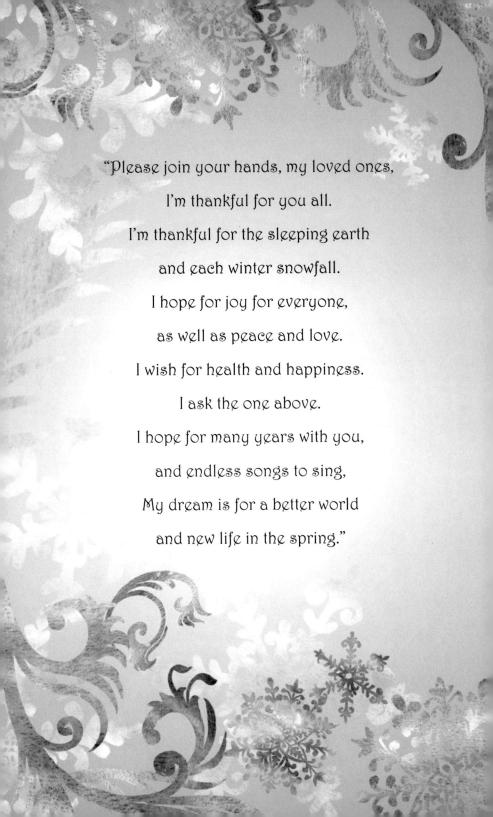

"Please join your hands, my loved ones,

I'm thankful for you all.

I'm thankful for the sleeping earth

and each winter snowfall.

I hope for joy for everyone,

as well as peace and love.

I wish for health and happiness.

I ask the one above.

I hope for many years with you,

and endless songs to sing,

My dream is for a better world

and new life in the spring."

The Fairy and
the Rabbit

Once upon a time, in a magical forest, snow fell on a tall mountain. Wind howled, whistling through the trees, making snowflakes dance in the air. Snow was everywhere, completely covering the ground. The mountain was peaceful. Many creatures of the forest slept soundly until spring would arrive. The cold mountain seemed empty, except for one spot. Near the top, a faint flicker of light shone from a small cave.

There was almost no sound at all by the small cave. Suddenly something ran quickly from the cave entrance. It was Sherwyn the rabbit. Sherwyn was brown and white, with fluffy fur and big floppy ears. Riding the rabbit was a wild-looking fairy named Raluca. Raluca was dressed in heavy winter clothes and had a bow and arrow on her back. They moved as fast as they could, skidding down the hill from side to side.

"Let's hop faster, Sherwyn. We have to visit Ackley the owl," said Raluca.

The two had a weekly appointment with Ackley to get updates on the forest. Ackley gave a report on such things as snowfall, wind speed and sun position. It was very informative. Also, each week, Ackley gave them a new assignment to help keep the forest safe.

Sherwyn and Raluca were considered the bravest fairy and animal team in the entire magical forest. Their weekly visit with Ackley was always interesting. Ackley liked to give them their assignments in rhyming riddles. It typically took half a week to figure out the riddle and the other half to complete the task. This week seemed to be no different.

"Hooloo to you," spouted Ackley from his hollow tree. "How are Sherwyn the Swift and Raluca the Radiant on this beautiful winter morning?"

"We're great, Ackley the Astute. It's a pleasure to see you, too," replied Raluca. The three laughed. They always liked to have a grand introduction before their weekly meeting.

"Have you prepared our assignment for the week?" asked Sherwyn.

"Yes, yes, of course," replied Ackley. "Ah hum."
Ackley always cleared his throat before his
performance of the rhyming riddle.

"There are two moons until the spring,
The coldest day, winter's yet to bring.
Find the future home for wings,
And take your findings to the King
Before the first songbird sings."

Ackley took a bow as Sherwyn and Raluca
looked at each other, scratching their heads.

"Go forth, brave ones," declared Ackley as he went back into his tree, closing his eyes as he nestled in for a nap.

Raluca climbed onto Sherwyn's back, and the two rode off. They returned to the cave to think about the riddle.

"It's a week's hop to the King," said Sherwyn.

"We should start now and figure out the riddle on the way," replied Raluca as she shoved clothing into a bag. 'The coldest day, winter's yet to bring' so we should pack warm. This cave is getting a bit chilly, too."

"What is the future home for wings?"
Sherwyn looked puzzled. "We will think of it
soon, I'm sure," said Sherwyn.

The two were packed, and at first light on
the next morning, they began their journey. It
would be a long voyage through the snow, but
Sherwyn and Raluca were brave and very
experienced in the harsh weather.

"We should search for some food, too," said Sherwyn. The two had packed food, but it's always good to have a bit extra when traveling in the winter woods.

"Smart idea, Sherwyn," said Raluca.

The two followed the path to the home of the King and the Queen, an enchanted tree nestled in the center of the magical forest. On the way they talked about the riddle, wondering what it could mean.

"There are two moons until the spring,
The coldest day, winter's yet to bring.
Find the future home for wings,
And take your findings to the King
Before the first songbird sings."

"Two moons can mean two months, I
think," said Sherwyn. "It is still two more
months until spring."

"And we are already heading to the King," added Raluca. "There are just a few more parts to solve. I hope that we make it home before the coldest day of winter. Ackley sure sent us far this time."

"Now we need to find the future home for wings," said Sherwyn. "That one is tough."

For days, the two trudged through snow and over icy rocks. The frozen terrain made it difficult to find food. Occasionally, one of them would find a seed pod or nut and add it to their bag as a reserve. Each night, they curled up to stay warm. They hoped that the next day they would find the answer to Ackley's riddle. As they were falling asleep, they talked about how wonderful it would be to meet the King.

On the sixth day, the two were no closer to solving the riddle. The days were getting colder and their food supply was running low. There was enough food for two more days but they continued picking up seeds and nuts when they found them.

"Look! An acorn," shouted Raluca pointing up to an acorn hanging from a bare branch. She pulled back an arrow on her bow, aimed carefully and knocked the acorn to the ground. "Add this to the bag, Sherwyn!"

The bag now had 35 thistle seeds, 27 grass seeds, 5 frozen raspberries, 4 acorns and 3 hickory nuts. It was all they had to show for their journey so far. They still hadn't found the future home for wings, and it was only a short distance until they arrived at the enchanted tree of the King.

The last day was the coldest yet. Dark clouds filled the sky, and heavy snow fell. It was hard to see anything. The two brave companions continued on to the enchanted tree despite having failed their mission. They entered the door and were prepared to apologize to the King.

When they walked through the door, a huge crowd of fairies and animals roared with applause. They were cheering and clapping at their arrival. The two were very confused.

"Congratulations, Sherwyn the Swift and Raluca the Radiant, you have made it safely before the coldest day of winter. Please rest here until the mighty storm passes," exclaimed the King.

From high in the tree, the sound of a songbird echoed through the hall. A bird swooped down and wrapped her wings around the fairy and the rabbit.

"Thank you for your brave journey," said the bird.

"We must apologize," replied Raluca. "We did not find the future home for wings. We are sorry."

"Nonsense," exclaimed the King. "Open your bag." Raluca opened up the bag of seeds, nuts and berries they collected along the way.

"Fantastic! We know right where to plant them," said the King. "In the spring the seeds will be planted and in just a few years, it will be a perfect home for birds. The thistle and berries will provide food for birds to eat. The grass will grow and spread and become material that birds can use to build homes. The acorns and hickory nuts will become mighty trees with branches so birds can create their nests. These are the homes for wings. Thank you!"

Raluca and Sherwyn blushed; they had no idea that they had solved the riddle. They were relieved that the King was pleased. As they turned around, they saw a familiar face. It was Ackley, looking upon them and smiling.

"Ackley, that was quite the riddle," said Sherwyn.

"You solved it beautifully, as always," replied Ackley. "I knew it all along. Also, I kept my friends out of the storm. I think the enchanted tree is much warmer than your cave. And, you helped my feathered friends, too. I think it was a good riddle. Now let me tell you the riddle for this week."

The three friends laughed. They were not ready for another challenge so soon.

They all stayed in the enchanted tree until the storm had passed and the coldest day of winter was gone. When the sun came out again, the trio traveled back to the mountain. Along the way, Sherwyn and Raluca collected more seeds and nuts to plant by the cave where they lived, as Ackley recited his rhyming riddles.

Molezart

Once upon a time, deep in a Magical Forest, there lived a mole. His name was Molezart. He was no ordinary mole. He was a musical mole. Molezart loved classical music and would sing and write songs as he dug through his tunnels. Molezart would often poke his head out of his mole hole when the forest band had its concerts so he could listen to the beautiful music.

He wanted very much to become the conductor of the forest band. He admired Myra the fairy, Cora the bird, Randall the rabbit and Murray the turtle. He especially admired Mrs. Cranberry, the most famous member of the Magical Forest band. He even had her picture on his tunnel wall. He wished more than anything that the entire magical forest could hear his music. But moles stay underground, so how could anyone hear his music? He was afraid his dream would never come true.

Molezart knew if he were to ever fulfill his dream, he would need to get help. So he decided to tunnel to the enchanted tree to ask the fairy King and Queen for guidance. He told King Noble and Queen Grace of his hope that the entire magical forest could hear his music. The royal couple loved the idea and advised Molezart on how to achieve his goal.

"You must go on a journey, Molezart. Travel north, south, east and west, in any order you wish. If all corners of the forest want to hear your music, then you will be named the King's conductor and the hollow cave near our enchanted tree will become your concert hall. After each leg of your journey, come back to the hollow cave as it will give you inspiration to continue. Seeing your future concert hall will give you the strength for the next day," said the King. Molezart happily agreed and set off on his quest. He never imagined that he could be the King's conductor, with his own concert hall.

Molezart stuck his nose to the ground and wiggled himself under the dirt. He first headed to the eastern woods to ask the forest band if it would perform in his future concert hall. As he burrowed in the ground, he sang and hummed his songs, eager to write more tunes for the upcoming concerts. As he came out of his new tunnel, he was greeted by his idol, Mrs. Cranberry. She was the lead singer of the band. Molezart shared his dream of having the whole forest hear his music. The Magical Forest band was very excited and all members agreed to play any song that Molezart wrote.

Molezart excitedly burrowed back into the new tunnel, which led back to the site of the future concert hall. He looked into the entrance of the hollow cave and pictured himself conducting the forest band in front of a large audience of animals and fairies.

The next morning, Molezart started digging his next tunnel, this time heading west. He dug a tunnel to the oak grove where Fuzzy the mouse lived. Once again, he hummed his new songs and imagined musical notes flying through the air.

He found Fuzzy and his fairy friend Dizzy jumping in a leaf pile. Molezart shared his goal of a having the entire magical forest hear his music. Dizzy and Fuzzy were very excited about this prospect and encouraged the musical mole on his pursuit. Fuzzy even offered to help decorate the stage.

Delighted by the support, Molezart rushed down the tunnel to see the hollow cave and to report his progress to the King and Queen. The enchanted tree where the royal couple lived was near the cave. Molezart first viewed the cave for inspiration. He waved an imaginary baton and pictured a full audience. He then tunneled to the enchanted tree to give a full report. The King and Queen encouraged Molezart and congratulated him for being halfway done with his journey. They reminded him that if the others in the forest were interested in hearing the music he would have his concert hall.

Molezart started a new tunnel, this time heading south to the pond. He was getting tired from digging tunnels. Even for a mole, this was a lot of digging. He decided to rest when his tunnel crossed with another. Molezart had tunneled right to the intersection of Chipmunk Circle and Squirrel Street. It was a busy section below the forest floor with carts in a row and vendors selling acorns, seeds and more.

Molezart thought about his new tunnels and realized he could use them to travel to his parent's home on Mole Hill Heights. He would just need to travel a bit down Squirrel Street, take a left onto Beetle Boulevard then a right onto Woodchuck Way. He was glad that his tunnels now connected so much of the Magical Forest with the future concert hall.

When he was rested, Molezart got back up and started digging. He sang while he worked and heard the echo of his voice.

"These tunnels have great acoustics," exclaimed Molezart as he continued his tune.

"Digging, digging down, across the town, they hear my sound, all around, the sound is found," he sang.

When he reached the edge of the pond, he found Kicker the frog and Gideon the fairy lying on lily pads staring at the sky. Molezart told them the plan for the concert hall and that the forest band would perform the songs he wrote. The two agreed that music would be a nice treat as they relaxed on the water. The two seemed to be more interested looking at shapes in the clouds and unwinding at the moment. Molezart supposed even great adventurers like Gideon and Kicker needed a break sometimes.

"Have a rest, Molezart , you have travelled far" said Gideon.

"Maybe a bath," croaked Kicker.

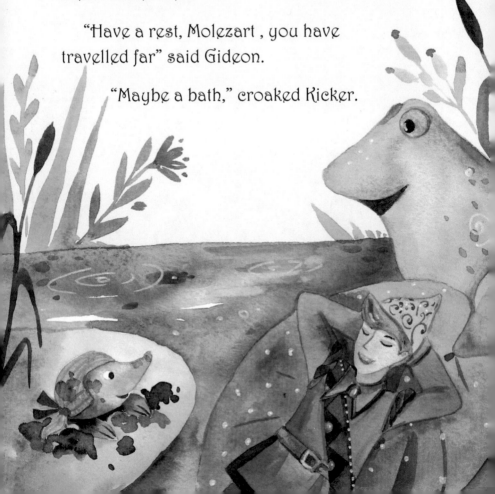

Even for an underground animal, Molezart was particularly dirty from digging. Molezart took a few steps back to get a running start to the pond.

"Mole Dive," he shouted, as he leapt into the air. He made a great splash, causing ripples in the pond and soaking Gideon and Kicker with water.

Kicker let out a load bellowing: "CROAK."

"That's a nice sound, Kicker," joked Molezart. "Perhaps you can join the Magical Forest band."

After Molezart's swim, Kicker and Gideon wished him good luck on his quest and said they looked forward to many concerts to come.

Molezart got back to the hollow cave through the fresh tunnel he had dug. He was glad his journey was almost over but knew the trip to the winter mountain would be the most difficult yet.

He started early the next morning. Although he had a relaxing break swimming the day before, his muscles were tired and his claws were sore from digging. As he got farther north, the soil got colder and his musical notes seemed to get a bit longer and slower as he sang. He was exhausted after a full day of tunneling when he broke through the snow on the top of the Winter Mountain by the cave of Ralucca the fairy and Sherwyn the rabbit.

He sat with them in the cave as he explained the concert hall and his dream of having the entire forest hear his music. The two thought the idea was great, but they did not understand how music would reach all the way up to their mountain home. Molezart felt discouraged as he crawled back into the underground tunnel. He had no idea how it would work either. He hoped the King would still allow him to be his conductor.

As Molezart climbed back into the tunnel, he thought he heard someone's voice in the long hole.

"My ears must be frozen," thought Molezart, "there is no one nearby for miles. Molezart burrowed back down the long tunnel from the winter mountain to the hollow cave. He got to the end of the tunnel where he found the King and Queen waiting for him. With them were Mrs. Cranberry and the rest of the Magical Forest band waiting to perform. The hollow cave had been transformed into a beautiful concert hall.

"Congratulations, Molezart. You did it. You are now the King's conductor," said Queen Grace.

"We are so proud of you, Molezart. Now take the stage and conduct your band," added King Noble, handing him his very own conductor's baton. Molezart was very happy but didn't understand who the concert was for. There was no one in the audience. Nonetheless, he took his place in front of the band. He tapped his conductor's baton and, as he lifted it in the air, the band began to play.

As the musical notes filled the air, they traveled down each of the four tunnels Molezart had dug. All of the animals and fairies that Molezart visited could hear the music through his tunnels. As the music reached all over the forest, the animals and fairies all stopped and listened to the beautiful sound. Molezart had made his dream come true. He was now the King's conductor, and by his own hard work, he had made it possible for the entire Magical Forest to hear his music.

The End

Irina Zatica Trzaskos is the illustrator of *Tales From a Magical Forest*. Irina was born in Moldova and moved to the United States in 2012. Her unique style mixes the latest creative artistic trends with traditional European charm. Her artwork has been licensed for use on many home décor items worldwide. You can join Irina's watercolor classes for beginners following the link below.

www.skillshare.com/r/irinatrzaskos

Justin Frank Trzaskos is the author of *Tales From a Magical Forest*. The books were inspired by his wife's colorful and creative artwork. The fairies for *A Fairy Christmas Eve* started as a watercolor holiday print, which soon evolved into the entire book series. Irina and Justin met as counselors at Camp J.N.Webster in Ashford, Connecticut; the memories of those summer days sparked *Welcome to Camp Summmberberry*. Justin was born in Coventry, Connecticut, where the couple still resides today. The *Tales From a Magical Forest* book series was a project that took five years to create. *The Fairy and The Frog* was published in 2014, and the seven-book series was completed in 2019.

Tales From a Magical Forest

Books by Justin and Irina Trzaskos

The Fairy and the Frog

The Fairy and the Bird

The Fairy and the Mouse

The Fairy and the Rabbit

A Fairy Christmas Eve

Welcome to Camp Summerberry

Molezart

Tales From a Magical Forest Coloring Book

Tales From a Magical Forest – seven books in one

www.facebook.com/talesfromamagicalforest

www.amazon.com/author/talesfromamagicalforest